# THE
# BEDSPREAD
## by Sylvia Fair

William Morrow and Company
New York 1982

Library of Congress Cataloging in Publication Data

Fair, Sylvia.
    The bedspread.
Summary: Two elderly sisters embroider the home of their childhood at either end
of a white bedspread, each as she remembers it, with results that surprise them.
[1. Embroidery—Fiction] I. Title.            PZ7.F146Be    [E]    81-11152
ISBN 0-688-00877-1                                              AACR2

For Iola

Once, in a long, long bed, lived two old, old sisters.
They ate their meals in bed, washed their faces in bed,
and at night they slept in their long, long bed.

"I'm fed up," complained Maud.

"You're not half as fed up as I am," replied Amelia sulkily.

"Oh, yes, I am," insisted Maud. "It's that clock, ticking all the time."

"No, it isn't," argued Amelia. "It's that wallpaper. Every rose is the same as the next."

"No, it's not."

"Yes, it is."

"No, it's not."

"And the worst thing of all," said Amelia,
"is this boring white bedspread."

Maud looked down at the boring white bedspread,
and for once in her long life she agreed with Amelia.

"Amelia!" she said sharply. "If this white bedspread
is so very boring, then we should decorate it."

And, for once in her long life, Amelia
agreed with Maud.

They rummaged under the bed until they
found their old workbaskets and opened
them. They were full of scissors and thimbles,
pins and needles, buttons and bodkins, and
hooks and eyes. There were scraps of silk and
satin, rolls of ribbon, lengths of lace.

"Look!" exclaimed Maud. "My thimble
still fits."

"And so do my scissors," said Amelia,
snipping excitedly at the air.

Eagerly they threaded their needles, then

stopped. They didn't know what to sew. They stared empty faced at one another ... until Amelia had an idea.

"Do you remember the house we lived in as children?" she asked breathlessly.

"Do you remember the stitches we were taught at school?" asked Maud severely.

"Let's embroider a picture of our old house," suggested Amelia brightly.

"And let's see how many different stitches we can work into it," agreed Maud. "We'll each make a house, one at each end of the bedspread. Then it will be symmetrical."

Maud measured the bedspread and marked the exact center with a safety pin. "Now listen, Amelia," she said. "Your house mustn't come past that pin."

Amelia nodded understandingly as she fumbled in the workbasket on her knee.

"And we'll begin at the front door," decided Maud.

"A very good place to start, dear," said Amelia with a smile.

And so they began to sew. *Snicketty-snack* went their little
silver scissors, and *picketty-pick* went their sharp needles as
they cut and stitched, cut and stitched.

"There were five stone steps up to the front door,"
Amelia remembered, "and a black cat called Ferdinand used
to slink along the railings."

"Don't make the railings crooked," warned Maud.

"But they *were* crooked, Maud!"

The doors of their houses grew.

Maud cut a neat oblong of purple velvet for her door and worked each panel in fine spider stitch. She made the railings of hairpin lace and crocheted a half-moon for the fanlight over the door.

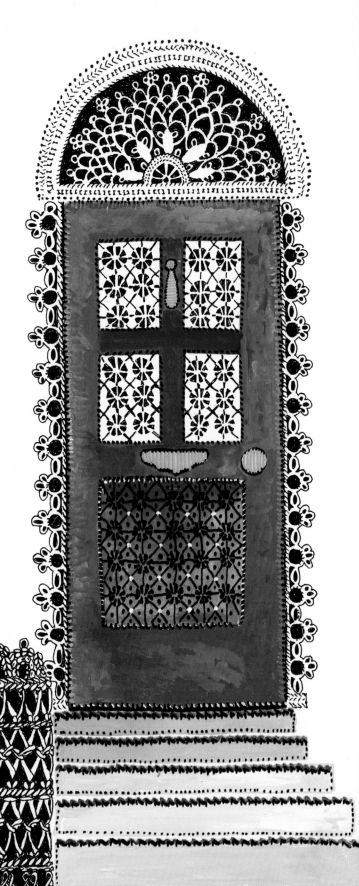

Amelia made her door from
the pocket of an old blue dress
and cut the steps out of a pair of
old fawn underdrawers.

She found a brass button for
the doorknob, a buckle for the
letter box, and a curtain ring for
the knocker. And since she
couldn't remember any of her
stitches, she had to invent them as
she went along.

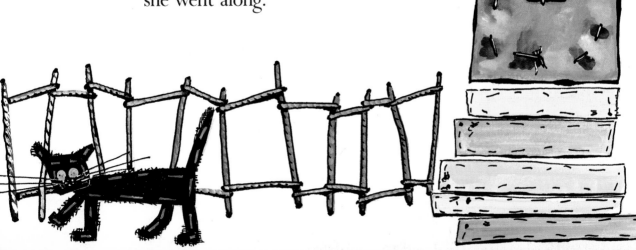

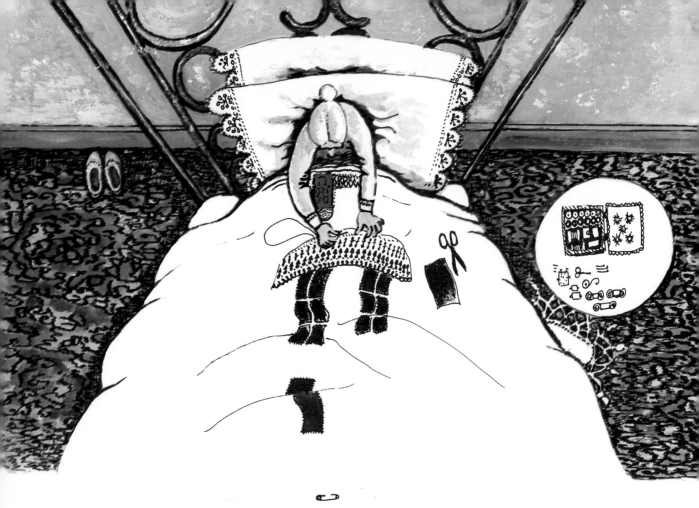

On Tuesday, Maud said, "Today we will make the
windows. And don't forget the balcony on the first floor."

All day they snipped and stitched, snipped and stitched,
so that when it was time to go to sleep, the windows were
finished.

Maud cut squares of satin for her windowpanes and
framed them in buttonhole stitch. She chose pearl thread
for the balcony rail and wove it into lozenges of knots with
intercrossed bars.

Amelia's windows were crooked and frayed, and they were framed in string that wouldn't lie flat. But flowers bloomed in window boxes on every floor, and on the balcony she stitched herself with Maud, and their father and mother, and all their brothers and sisters.

On Wednesday, Maud said, "Today we shall make the walls."
Maud cut three hundred and twenty-six calico bricks and
whipped them into place with invisible stitches.
"You haven't missed a single brick!" marveled Amelia.
She hadn't even tried to build her wall of bricks. She had
only remembered the creeper full of flycatchers' nests and the
vine that was so easy to climb down secretly by moonlight.

On Thursday, Maud said,
"Today we shall stitch the roof."
She found a tortoiseshell
crochet hook and worked ten
rows of tiles in pineapple stitch.

But Amelia only remembered
the time when three peacocks
from the nearby park had roosted
on the roof and cried "Help!" in
the middle of the night.

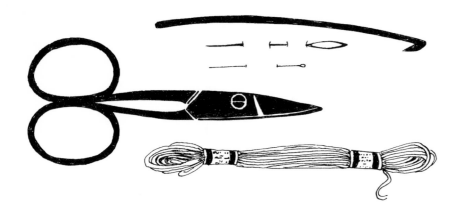

On Friday, Maud said, "Today
we will build the chimneys."

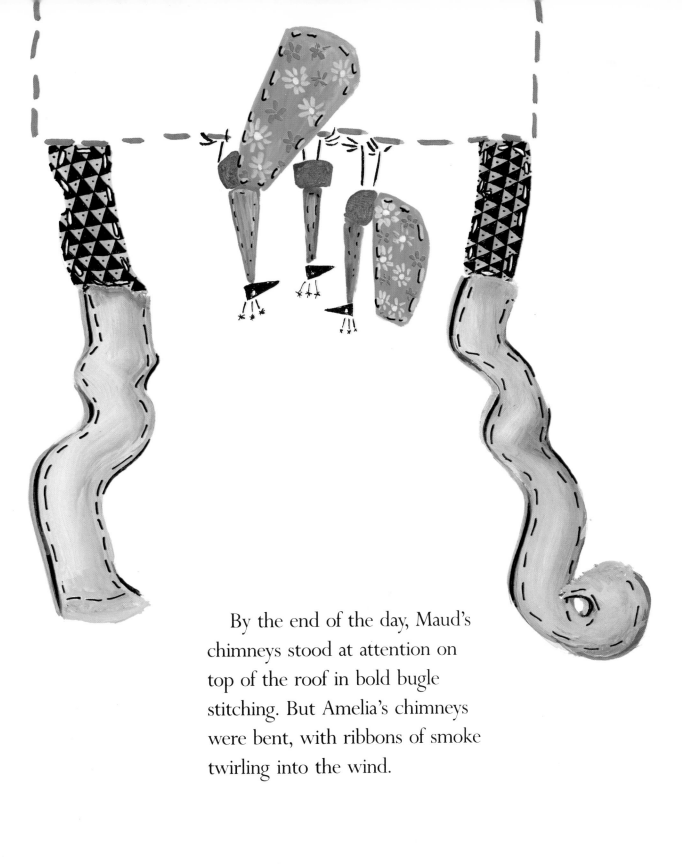

By the end of the day, Maud's chimneys stood at attention on top of the roof in bold bugle stitching. But Amelia's chimneys were bent, with ribbons of smoke twirling into the wind.

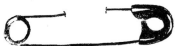

On Saturday, Maud said, "Well, that's finished."

"But we haven't done the garden yet!" Amelia protested.

"The garden was in the back," Maud reminded her.

"I want to sew the garden," said Amelia stubbornly.

So they agreed to make a garden each.

Maud worked a pretty border of flowers in raised satin stitch. But Amelia's garden was like a jungle, with trees to climb and a swing in the apple tree.

At the end of the day, Maud looked at the bedspread
and smiled. "This time it really *is* finished," she said firmly.
"Tomorrow is Sunday. We never sew on Sundays."
So they went to sleep, happy under their houses.

On Sunday, Maud said, "Today we will turn the bedspread around, so that I can see your house and you can see mine."

So they turned the bedspread carefully around and saw at once that it was not symmetrical at all.

"I--I'm afraid my stitching isn't quite as tidy as yours," stammered Amelia guiltily. "I'd forgotten my stitches."

"But your house is happy," said Maud rather sadly. "I had forgotten the happiness."

They turned the bedspread back again, so that Amelia could look at her own happy house and Maud at her beautifully stitched one.

"We haven't done the sky!" said Amelia suddenly.

"No sewing on Sunday," said Maud.

A picture should have the sun in it, thought Amelia. The sun shone every day when I was a child.

So when Maud was snoozing after dinner, Amelia secretly cut out a golden circle of satin sunshine. Silently she unfastened the safety pin and stitched the sun in its place.

When Maud awoke, she noticed that her house was looking brighter, and she felt brighter too. She didn't even scold Amelia for overlapping the sun onto her half or even for sewing on a Sunday.

"So that's finished," said Maud on Monday.

They put away their workbaskets, and they fiddled and twitched, not knowing what to do with themselves.

"There's plenty more space left on the bedspread," Amelia hinted.

"And plenty of stitches we haven't used yet!"

So they took out their workbaskets again, opened them, and once more began to sew.

And this time they never stopped. Amelia remembered the muffin man, roasted chestnuts, and hopscotch on the pavement.

Maud remembered the fern stitch, rice stitch, and fishbone stitch.

Then, when they were about a hundred and three years old, the sisters died and their bedspread was put in a museum for all to see.

On Mondays, Wednesdays, and Fridays it is hung so that Maud's house is right side up; on Tuesdays, Thursdays, and Saturdays it is hung so that Amelia's house is right side up. On Sundays, the museum is closed.